SHHHHHH...my name is Marvin!

I love my yellow kayak,
it's hiding in my room.
Mom and Dad don't know it's up here,
I'd better tell them soon.

I climb into my kayak,
close my eyes and dream.
After zipping up my life jacket,
I start paddling down the stream.

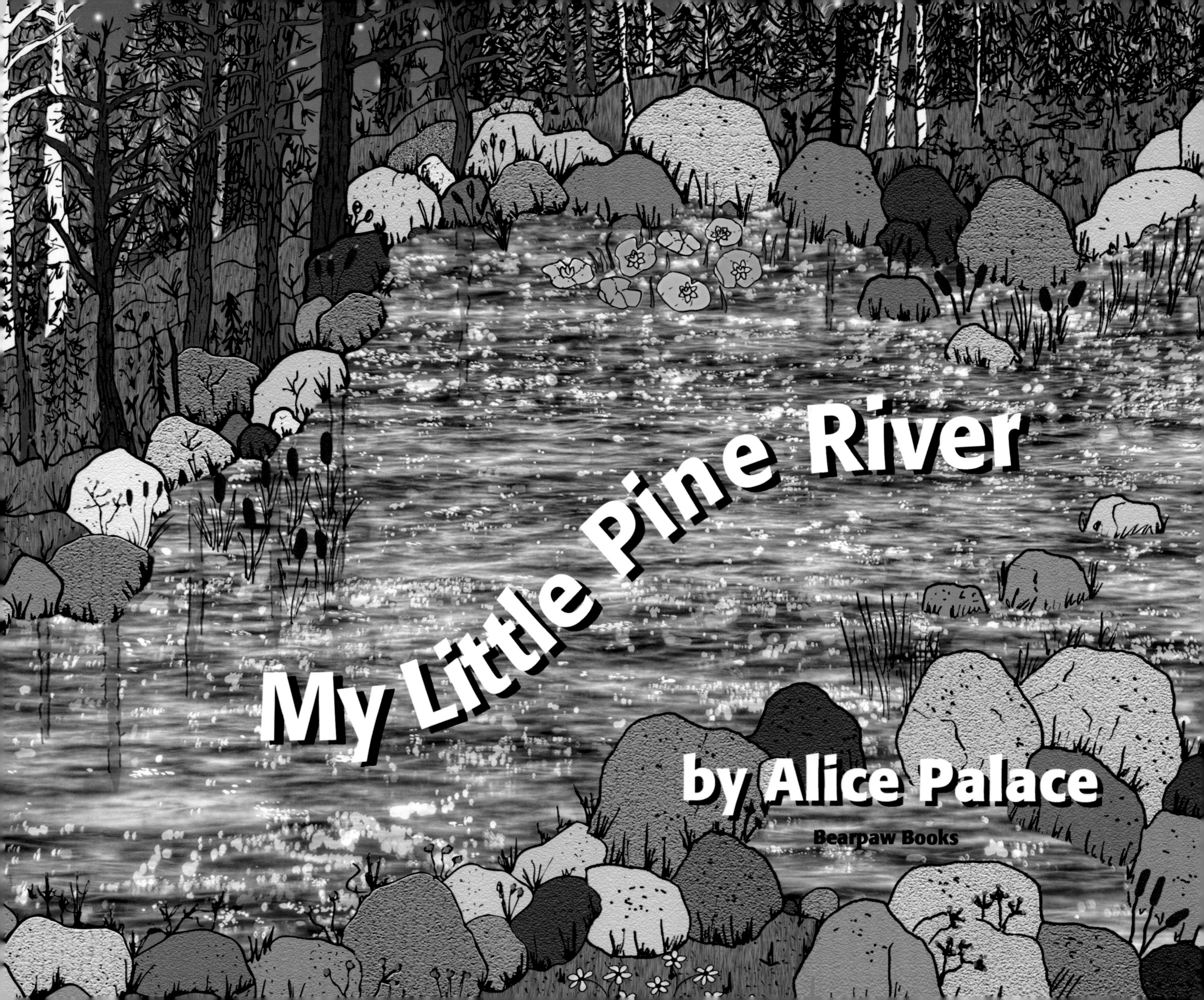
My Little Pine River
by Alice Palace
Bearpaw Books

I'm paddling down the river,
and what do I see?

I see a monarch butterfly,
fluttering over me.

Landing on a cattail,
he flaps his bright orange wings.
After resting, he flies away
landing on other things.

I'm paddling down the river,
and what do I see?

I see a fisherman
with his lure up in a tree.

He pulls, shakes and tugs,
suddenly the fly is free.
A hungry trout takes the bait,
and jumps in front of me!

I'm paddling down the river,
and what do I see?

I see a kingfisher
soaring high and so free.

Suddenly, he dives down
to find something to eat.
Bobbing up again,
he catches a wiggly treat.

I'm paddling down the river,
and what do I see?

I see a wooden bridge
high up over me.

Gliding slowly under,
I look above and see
a great big, spooky spider
staring down at me.
YOWEEE!

I'm paddling down the river,
and what do I see?

I see a dragonfly
landing on my knee.

If I'm very quiet,
I think he'll want to stay,
but he waves his wings to say goodbye,
then quickly flies away.

I'm paddling down the river,
and what do I see?
I see a rocky cave
in the hill beside a tree.

I paddle in very slowly,
it's dark and hard to see.
Oh, oh! I'm not alone in here,
eyes are watching me.
Eeeeeeeek!

I'm paddling down the river,
and what do I see?

I see wood ducks
swimming in front of me.

With colorful feathers
all black, white and green,
they bob their heads as they swim
down the winding stream.

I'm paddling down the river,
and what do I see?

I see an old mill
on the shore next to me.

The paddle wheel is turning,
'round and 'round it goes.
Scooping up the water,
over the top it flows.

I'm paddling down the river,
and what do I see?

I see a painted turtle
sunning on a tree.

Her shell is warm and toasty
from sleeping in the sun.
She slides into the water
when her quiet nap is done.

I'm paddling down the river,
and what do I see?

I see an island
right in front of me.
I glide my kayak up,
and land on the sandy shore.

Then I build a small campfire,
and roast myself a s'more.
Yumm! Yumm!

Grahams
HONEY
HERSHEY'S
Milk Chocolate
HERSHEY'S
Milk Chocolate
HERSHEY'S
Milk Chocolate

I'm paddling down the river,
and what do I see?

I see a great blue heron
fishing close to me.

Her neck is long and narrow,
and her legs straight and tall.
Catching a fish in her bill,
she swallows it tail and all.

I'm paddling down the river,
and what do I see?

OH, NO!
I see a bubbling rapids,
churning in front of me.
Grahams

I get my paddle ready,
and move slowly to the edge.
When I'm really close,
I push over the watery ledge!

YA-HOOOOO!

Grahams
HONEY
HERSHEY'S
Milk Chocolate
HERSHEY'S
Milk Chocolate
HERSHEY'S
Milk Chocolate

Whew! I open my eyes,
and remember too soon,
my kayaking adventure
was really in my room!

I better go to sleep now,
and dream about my ride.
I love my yellow kayak,
I'm still hiding it inside.

Good night yellow kayak!
Good night river friends!

My Little Pine River

ISBN 0-9709444-3-8
LCCN TXu 1-227-819

Graphic Design and Illustrations Colorized by Carrie Smeby and Nancy Hendrickson
Creative Collaboration with Mary Anderson
Technical Assistance by Pamela Costello

A special thank you to:
Hershey Food Corporation – www.hersheys.com
"The Hershey's trademark & trade dress are trademarks used with permission of Hershey Food Corporation"
Hoigaard's – www.hoigaards.com
Keebler - www.keebler.com
Walden Kayaks
Wenonah for their Cadence paddle – www.wenonah.com

For more information contact:
Bearpaw Books
P. O. Box 122
Emily, MN 56447
www.bearpawbooks.com

Enjoy all Alice Palace books:
Adventure One, **My Little Cabin** *Adventure Two,* **My Little Lighthouse**
Adventure Three, **My Little Fish House** *Adventure Four,* **My Little Pine River**
Adventure Five, **My Little Sailboat** *Adventure Six,* **My Little Mountain**

Printed and bound in the United States of America by:
Bang Printing, Brainerd, Minnesota